PRESENTED TO:

ANIMAL LOVER'S NAME

FROM

DATE

MORE PAWVERBS FOR KIDS

more PAWVERBS™ ~ for Kids ~

30 More Heartwarming Stories about Boys, Girls, and Their Pets

JENNIFER MARSHALL BLEAKLEY

TYNDALE KIDS

Tyndale House Publishers

CAROL STREAM, ILLINOIS

Visit Tyndale's website for kids at tyndale.com/kids.

Tyndale is a registered trademark of Tyndale House Ministries. The Tyndale Kids logo is a trademark of Tyndale House Ministries.

Pawverbs is a trademark of Jennifer Marshall Bleakley.

More Pawverbs for Kids: 30 More Heartwarming Stories about Boys, Girls, and Their Pets

Designed by Ron C. Kaufmann

Published in association with Jessica Kirkland and the literary agency of Kirkland Media Management, LLC.

For information about special discounts for bulk purchases, please contact Tyndale House Publishers at csresponse@tyndale.com, or call 1-855-277-9400.

Library of Congress Cataloging-in-Publication Data

A catalog record for this book is available from the Library of Congress.

ISBN 978-1-4964-8408-6

Printed in China

30 29 28 27 26 25 24
7 6 5 4 3 2 1

For Andrew and Ella: I still love you forever times infinity—and I always will!

A Note from the Author

HI! MY NAME IS JEN, and I like animals—a lot. I like watching animals, playing with them, and learning about them. I think they are funny and cute and interesting. But what I love most about animals is how they help me think about and learn about God.

Did you know that animals can do that?

It's true!

If you slow down, pay attention, and ask God for help—you can learn things about *him* from the animals he created.

One of the most important things I've learned from animals is that I can talk to God as easily as I can talk to an animal.

You see, I was what you would call a shy kid. Talking to people, sometimes even to my friends, felt scary. Talking to teachers and doctors and other grown-ups was especially hard. My hands would get sweaty, and my stomach would hurt. I wanted to talk to people. I wished I could just open my mouth and talk as easily as my friends did, but it was hard, and I often felt lonely.

One day when I was sitting outside, my cat, Sugar, walked over to me and climbed onto my lap. She started purring.

"You make me feel happy and safe, Sugar," I said,

rubbing my hand back and forth on her gray-and-black fur.

I started talking to Sugar while I petted her. I told her about a hard test I had taken at school, about a friend who'd hurt my feelings, and how I wished I could try out for the school play—but that I was too scared. Sugar kept purring. She was so easy to talk to that all the words I had been holding in for a long time came out.

The next day, I went to find Sugar as soon as I got home from school. I told her that I got an okay grade on the test, made up with my friend, and signed up to be in the chorus for the school play—so I could be in the play but didn't have to try out for a speaking part. Sugar listened and purred.

The next Sunday at church, our pastor talked about the ways God cares for us. He read a verse from 1 Peter that says, "Give all your worries and cares to God, for he cares about you" (5:7). When he read that verse, I thought about Sugar and how she listened to all my worries and the things I cared about.

Later that day, while Sugar purred on my lap, I started talking to God—telling him how much I wanted to be able to talk to other people, thanking him for bringing Sugar into my life, and asking him to help me not feel so scared all the time.

That day, I realized that God was with me, like Sugar was with me—but that God was even better because he is *always* with me. Sugar couldn't go to school or to the doctor's office with me, but God could. And he did.

Sugar helped me learn that I can talk to God, and God helped me not feel as scared all the time. Sometimes I still get a little scared when I have to talk to someone new, but now I know I can talk to God about that—and he will help me.

And that's why I wrote this book. I wrote it so I would remember all the things I've learned, and I wrote it so that *you* can learn things from animals too—things about yourself, about other people, and about God.

Each story in this book is based on something that actually happened with a real animal. There is a Paws and Ponder section after each story with questions to answer so you can learn your own lessons from the animals. And there is a Paws and Pray section with a short prayer too.

You can read one story at a time or read lots of stories at once. You can read the book at bedtime or in the morning or in the afternoon. You can read the stories with your family, with a friend, by yourself, or to your pet. However you decide to read this book, I hope you will enjoy the stories and get to know God a little better through them.

Most of all, I hope you will come to know that God made you and loves you, and he thinks that you are very, very special—just the way you are.

And I think you're pretty PAWsome too!

Love, Jen

Hi, Donnie

When you please the LORD,
you can make your enemies into friends.

PROVERBS 16:7, GNT

JENNIE DIDN'T WANT to be scared of dogs. She tried really hard to be brave whenever she saw one. But their teeth looked so pointy and their claws looked so sharp, that no matter how hard she tried, she always ended up feeling afraid when she saw a dog.

Thankfully, she didn't see that many.

There were no dogs at her house.

No dogs at her school.

And no dogs at her church.

But there was one place—one place she loved going—where she would often see a dog.

Her grandparents' house.

Jennie's Uncle Ron and Aunt Nancy had a big German shepherd named Donnie. They liked to bring him with them to family picnics at her grandparents' house. Everyone in Jennie's family liked when Donnie came to visit—except Jennie.

Jennie's family knew she was scared of dogs, so they kept Donnie outside when she was there. That helped a little. But since Jennie's cousins weren't afraid of Donnie, they always went outside and played with him—and Jennie felt alone.

One summer day, when the family gathered at her grandparents' house for a picnic, Jennie watched from inside the house while her cousins played with Donnie.

Her cousin Mike threw a tennis ball for Donnie to catch.

Her cousins Becky and Tish pretended to shake Donnie's paw.

Her cousin Karen rubbed Donnie's belly when he lay down.

They looked like they were having so much fun. Jennie wanted to have fun too. She didn't want to be scared anymore.

Jennie took a deep breath.

She asked God to help her be brave.

And then she walked to the back door.

When Uncle Ron saw her, he smiled and said he would take Donnie inside.

"It's okay," Jennie whispered. *I'm okay*, she said to herself.

Jennie started to walk toward the big dog, who was lying on his back in front of her cousins.

"Come on over," Mike said.

Jennie inched her way forward.

What if Donnie jumps on me? What if he chases me? What if . . .

Donnie raised his big head. His dark eyes looked right at Jennie. She held her breath. Donnie's long tail made a thumping noise on the ground as he wagged it.

"That's his way of saying hi," Mike said.

"Hi, Donnie," Jennie said quietly.

She knelt down beside Mike. She took another deep breath. And she put her hand on Donnie's side. His fur felt soft and warm. His tongue stretched out of his mouth. His two front paws rested in her cousins' hands.

Donnie didn't look scary anymore.

He looked like a friend.

After that day, Jennie loved spending time with Donnie. He helped her not feel scared of dogs anymore. And he even made her think that someday she might like to have a dog of her own.

PAWS AND PONDER

Have you ever been afraid of something like Jennie was afraid of Donnie? What did you do?

Can you think of a time when feeling afraid might help you stay safe?

How did Jennie's family help her overcome her fear?

How could you help someone who feels afraid?

Paws and Pray

Dear God, please help me to be brave and talk to someone I trust when I feel afraid. Help me to also remember that I can talk to you about my feelings and you will always hear me.

Kelsey's Prayer

We can make our plans,
but the LORD determines our steps.

PROVERBS 16:9

KELSEY HAD ALWAYS WANTED a big dog. But when her dad lost his job and their family had to move into a small apartment to save money, she knew it would be a long time before they could get a big dog—or any dog.

She tried not to think about it, but whenever she saw big dogs at the park, she felt sad inside.

One day at church, the pastor told a story from the Bible about a little girl who was very sick. Her father ran to find Jesus. He begged Jesus to come to his house and heal his little girl. But as they were walking there, the little girl died. Kelsey's heart dropped. She imagined how sad the girl's dad must have felt. But then the pastor said something amazing. He said that Jesus

went to the girl's house anyway, and he brought her back to life!

Wow! Kelsey thought. *Jesus can do anything.*

That night, when Kelsey said her prayers, she asked God to let her get a dog someday. She figured if he could bring someone back to life, getting a dog would be really easy for him.

But when weeks passed and no dog showed up at her door, Kelsey started to wonder.

Maybe God didn't hear me. Or maybe he doesn't want me to get a dog.

Another month passed.

One Saturday morning, Aunt Lisa called and invited Kelsey's family over for lunch. She said she needed Kelsey's help with something.

Kelsey couldn't imagine what kind of help Aunt Lisa needed from her.

It only took twenty minutes to get to Aunt Lisa's house, but it felt like hours to Kelsey.

There was a strange van in the driveway.

"Did Aunt Lisa get a van?" Kelsey asked. Her mom and dad looked at each other and smiled.

"Nope," was all they said.

Instead of going to the front door like they usually did when they visited, Kelsey's dad led them to the backyard.

A woman Kelsey had never seen before was standing

over a giant open box. Aunt Lisa was kneeling in front of the box. When she saw Kelsey, she waved her over.

Puppies!

The box was full of little brown-and-white puppies.

Kelsey wanted to ask so many questions, but she was smiling too big to get any words out.

"I've been a bit lonely here," Aunt Lisa said, "so I thought maybe you could help me pick out a puppy to keep me company."

Kelsey was so excited. The puppies were so cute and so wiggly. She liked all of them, but her favorite was a small one with black, curly fur. Her aunt liked that puppy the best too. She named her Pippa.

"Thank you for helping me pick out Pippa," Aunt Lisa said. "And if it's okay with your parents, maybe you can come over every week and help me take care of her and play with her."

Kelsey gave her aunt a big hug. And as she played with Pippa, she realized that God really can do anything—even answer a prayer through someone else's dog.

PAWS AND PONDER

Have you ever asked God for something and felt like he didn't hear you?

Can you think of a time when God answered your prayer in a different way than you thought he would?

What do you think Kelsey learned about God in this story?

Paws and Pray

Dear God, help me to believe—and to remember—that you know what is best for me. Please help me trust you, especially when I really want something and have to wait.

Just the Way You Are

Kind words are like honey—sweet to the soul and healthy for the body.

PROVERBS 16:24

RILEY USUALLY SPOKE kind words to everyone, except herself. She wanted to be like everyone else so badly that whenever she felt different or thought she had messed up, she would say—and think—mean things about herself.

One day, her class went on a field trip to visit a big farm that grew lots of crops and had lots of animals. While they were there, she tried so hard to be funny and make jokes like Madison, to sound smart and recite animal facts like Zander, and to run as fast as Becca. But she messed up her joke, she didn't know any animal facts, and no one was as fast as Becca.

Why can't I have a special talent like everyone else? Riley thought to herself as their group walked over to see a small herd of rusty-brown horses after learning about growing corn.

The owner of the farm told them that four of the horses used to be racehorses. When the man waved a blue flag, the horses took off running. Their hooves sounded like thunder. They were so fast. The kids in Riley's class ran along the fence to get a closer look at the racehorses. But Riley noticed a big black horse standing by herself close to the fence.

"Why is that horse all alone?" Riley asked the farmer.

"That's Abby," he said. "She's a draft horse. She wasn't made to be fast. She was made to be strong and steady. Abby used to carry heavy loads for people. She's retired now—that's why she lives here. She seems to like it, but she can't keep up with the other horses when they start running like that."

Riley's heart did a funny flip-flop.

"Does she wish she could be fast like them?" she asked, pointing to the four galloping horses.

The farmer stared at Abby for a minute, then turned to look at Riley. "I sure hope not. 'Cause I like her just the way she is." The farmer nodded his head in Abby's direction. "You want to go say hi to her?"

Riley did.

"Hi, Abby," she said softly as she stepped closer to the big horse.

Abby stretched her head over the fence, and Riley put her hand on Abby's neck.

"It's okay not to be fast," Riley said, running her hand down Abby's black mane. "I like you just the way you are."

Abby's head bumped Riley's shoulder. And it felt like she was saying, *I like you just the way you are too.*

Riley's heart did the funny flip-flop thing again. And, for the first time in a long time, Riley was happy being Riley.

PAWS AND PONDER

Why do you think Riley's heart did a flip-flop when the farmer told her about Abby?

What type of words do you use when you talk to yourself?

Why is it important to use kind words when we speak to others—and to ourselves?

Paws and Pray

Dear God, thank you for loving me—and liking me—just the way I am. Please help me to use kind words when I talk to others and to use kind words when I think and speak about myself.

Boots's Bath

Love prospers when a fault is forgiven,
but dwelling on it separates close friends.

PROVERBS 17:9

KATIE WAS SO EXCITED to finally have her very own pet—an outdoor cat she named Boots. Katie didn't know much about cats, but when the stray cat kept coming to her back door and no one answered her missing cat signs, Katie's mom said she could keep him. Katie was so excited and promised her mom that she would take good care of Boots.

Most of Katie's friends had dogs. She knew one of the ways they took care of them was by giving them baths. So one hot summer day, Katie decided to give Boots a bath. She pulled out her old plastic kiddie pool and filled it with water.

But the moment Boots's paws touched the water,

the gray-and-black cat made a horrible screeching sound and tried to climb up Katie's arm.

"It's okay, Boots. It's just a bath. They're fun," Katie said, hoping Boots would believe her.

Katie kept one hand on Boots's squirmy back while she grabbed the shampoo bottle and squeezed. She squeezed so hard that the lid flew off and shampoo covered Boots.

Now her cat was mad and slippery.

Katie tried to rub the shampoo into Boots's fur, but the little cat slipped right through her hands, leapt out of the pool, jumped over the short fence, and raced down the street.

Katie cried.

She had just wanted to take care of her cat, but now he was lost and covered in shampoo.

Katie tried to find him, but Boots was gone.

"Just give him some time," Katie's mom said later that day. "Leave his food out, and he'll come back home when he's ready."

"But what if he never forgives me?" Katie asked. "What if he never wants to come back?"

Her mom hugged her. "Boots knows what a good friend you are. He will forgive you."

When two days passed with no sign of Boots, Katie thought her mom had been wrong. But on the third day—right after a big rainstorm—her cat came back.

"Boots, you're back!" Katie yelled when she spotted the cat on the deck. Katie ran outside. "I promise to never ever give you a bath again."

Boots rubbed his wet body against Katie's legs and purred. White shampoo suds covered Katie's legs.

Katie laughed. "From now on, I think I'll just let God wash you with the rain."

PAWS AND PONDER

Forgiving someone means letting go of our anger toward them. Why is it hard to forgive people sometimes?

Has someone ever forgiven you? How did that make you feel?

Is there someone you need to forgive today?

Paws and Pray

Dear God, thank you for forgiving me when I mess up. Please help me to forgive others, even when it's hard. And help me to be brave and ask for forgiveness from others when I haven't treated them the way I should.

A Friend for Trevor

A friend is always loyal, and a brother is born to help in time of need.

PROVERBS 17:17

TREVOR SAT BY HIMSELF. He didn't want to be at summer camp. He folded his arms over his stomach. The other kids were playing, and their happiness made him mad. Everything seemed to make Trevor mad these days.

All the other kids ran over to the basketball court to play four square, but Trevor didn't move.

He picked at some tall blades of grass. He kicked a rock. When he looked up, a big dog was standing in front of him.

A kind-looking lady was holding the dog's leash. She said her name was Ms. Sandee, and her sand-colored dog was Tesla. They would be spending the

week at camp too. Trevor had never heard of a dog going to camp before.

"This is Tesla's third time at camp," Ms. Sandee said.

Tesla sat down and put her head in Trevor's lap. Trevor touched her forehead with his finger.

"It's my *first* time," Trevor told Tesla.

Tesla held her paw up.

Trevor looked at Ms. Sandee.

"Tesla wants to shake your hand," she said.

Trevor shook Tesla's paw. "Nice to meet you, Tesla," he laughed.

Ms. Sandee asked Trevor if he would like to take her dog for a walk. He did. He took Tesla's leash and walked her over to a big field. He asked Ms. Sandee if he could run with Tesla. She said yes. Trevor started running, and Tesla ran too. She was really fast.

Trevor and Tesla spent every day of camp together. They went for walks, played fetch, and showed the other kids all the tricks Tesla could do. Tesla made camp a lot of fun. So much fun that Trevor wanted to come back next year.

"Ms. Sandee," Trevor asked as he helped her get Tesla in the car to go home, "do you think Tesla will remember me next year?"

Ms. Sandee's eyes got shiny as she answered, "I know she will remember. Tesla never forgets her friends."

"I love you, Tesla," Trevor whispered. "Thanks for being my friend."

PAWS AND PONDER

When was a time that you were mad like Trevor?
How did Tesla help Trevor feel better?
What made Tesla a good friend? How can you be a good friend like Tesla?

Paws and Pray

Dear God, sometimes I get really mad and really scared. Please remind me that you are always with me—even when I'm mad and scared. And help me remember that you are my friend.

The Birthday Surprise

A cheerful heart is good medicine, but a broken spirit saps a person's strength.

PROVERBS 17:22

"THIS IS GOING TO BE the worst birthday ever," Jackson told his dog, Max, the night before his birthday.

A big winter storm was coming, and his mom said they would have to reschedule his party because the roads would be too icy. Jackson didn't want anyone to get hurt, but he really wanted to play laser tag with his friends. He had felt so disappointed when his mom told him they couldn't even go out for dinner.

"I wish I had a summer birthday like my sister," Jackson told Max. "Her parties never have to get canceled because of icy roads."

Max laid his head on Jackson's stomach and sighed—it was almost as if his dog felt sad too.

Jackson rubbed Max's soft ears. He was glad his

family had adopted the two-year-old black Lab mix from the animal shelter last summer. He was fun to play with, and Jackson liked sharing his bed with Max—even though he took up a lot of room and liked to sleep with his head on Jackson's pillow!

Jackson fell asleep hugging his dog.

The next morning, Jackson woke up to more snow than he had ever seen. His backyard looked like a picture from one of the Christmas books his mom used to read to him. He threw off the covers and ran downstairs. Max raced after him.

His sister was already putting on her coat and gloves.

"Isn't it great!" she laughed.

Jackson was so excited that he forgot all about his party. He ran back upstairs to get his snow pants, then raced back downstairs. He shoved his arms into his coat, wiggled his fingers into his gloves, and searched through the hat basket until he found his favorite snow hat.

As he was putting it on, his mom and dad came around the corner. They were dressed for the snow too.

"You didn't think we were going to miss all the fun, did you?" Jackson's dad teased.

When his dad opened the back door, Max ran out. The black dog took four steps, then stopped. He lowered his head and sniffed the snow. He raised his head and sniffed the air. He looked at Jackson and tilted his head as if to say, *What is this?*

"The animal shelter said Max came from Florida," his mom said. "I bet he's never seen snow before."

Max took off running. He ran in circles. Then he stopped and started digging in the snow.

When Jackson threw a snowball, Max caught it in midair. Jackson laughed when Max ate the snowball.

Jackson and his sister spent the day making snowmen together, having snowball fights, and making snow angels. And as they did, Max ran around, barking happy barks and playing in the snow.

"This is the best birthday ever!" Jackson yelled while throwing another snowball for Max. "I am so glad my birthday is in January!"

PAWS AND PONDER

What does being disappointed feel like?

When have you felt disappointed? What helped you feel better?

How can you help someone who feels disappointed today?

Paws and Pray

Dear God, help me to remember that you are always with me—even on hard days when nothing feels like it's going right. Help me to remember that I can always talk to you when I'm disappointed, and that you love me no matter what.

Chief's Safe Place

The name of the LORD is a strong tower;
the righteous man runs into it and is safe.

PROVERBS 18:10, ESV

BOOM!

Thunder rumbled outside Madeline's house. It was a normal summer thunderstorm, but to Madeline's dog, Chief, it was the end of the world.

The yellow Lab jumped up from his favorite napping spot in the family room and ran to Madeline's parents' room—just like he did every time he got scared. Madeline set aside the picture she was drawing and went to check on Chief. His head and neck were hidden under her parents' bed, but the rest of his large, furry body was sticking out.

Another loud clap of thunder caused Madeline to jump. Chief whimpered.

"It's okay, Chief," Madeline said, sitting on the floor beside him. "I'll stay with you."

The next week was the Fourth of July. Madeline's family went to her grandparents' house to celebrate. They grilled hamburgers and hot dogs, made homemade ice cream, and played games outside. When it started to get dark, they drove to a park to watch a fireworks show.

"Chief?" Madeline's dad called out when they got home. "Where are you, buddy?"

Chief didn't run to greet them like he usually did. Madeline always liked how happy Chief was to see them when they got home. His tail would wag so fast that his whole body would wiggle. But this time there was no wagging tail. No wiggling dog. No Chief.

POP! POP! POP!

Madeline's neighbors were shooting off fireworks.

"Oh no. Poor Chief!" Madeline said, knowing how scared he must be.

Madeline and her parents found Chief hiding with his head under her parents' bed. Madeline's dad sat on one side of Chief, and she sat on the other. Chief's body was shaking with fear instead of wiggling from happiness.

"It's okay, boy," her dad said. "We're here now. And we will stay with you till the fireworks are over."

Madeline was glad Chief had somewhere to go

when he was scared. Somewhere that made him feel safe.

Madeline was too old to hide under her bed, but she did like staying close to her family—and to Chief—when she felt scared. And she also liked knowing that God was with her. It made her feel better to talk to him when something scared her—like shadows outside her window at night, scary dreams, or going to the dentist.

God didn't always stop the scary thing from happening, but he always stayed with her. And knowing she could run to God—like Chief ran to her parents' bed—made her feel a lot better.

PAWS AND PONDER

Where did Chief run when he got scared?

Where do you go when you feel scared?

How can we run to God if we can't see him?

What is something scary you can talk to God about today?

Paws and Pray

Dear God, you know there are a lot of things in this world that feel scary to me. When I feel that way, please help me remember that I can talk to you. And please help me be brave enough to talk to people I trust when I'm scared.

Chunky and the Cats

Friends come and friends go,
but a true friend sticks by you like family.

PROVERBS 18:24, MSG

WHEN HARPER'S DAD BROUGHT four kittens home to their farm, she didn't think she had ever seen anything cuter. Until he brought home ten baby chicks. The chicks were so small they fit in Harper's hand.

Harper had so much fun playing with the chicks and kittens. The kittens were only a little bigger than the baby chicks, and she loved watching them play together. When Harper wasn't at school, she was playing with the kittens and chicks.

As the kittens got bigger, they started exploring more of the farm. They met the goats, horses, donkey, and ducks. But they always raced back to the barn to play and snuggle with the chicks.

Harper was glad they were such good friends, but it also made her a little sad to see the kittens and chicks together.

"Anna and Vivi would have liked playing with you," Harper told her animal friends.

Anna and Vivi used to be Harper's best friends. But they were in different classes this year at school, and Anna and Vivi had made new friends and stopped talking to Harper. She missed them a lot. Her dad tried to make her feel better.

"Maybe you will meet a new best friend this year," he said.

But Harper didn't want new friends. She wanted her old friends back.

A few months after the kittens and chicks joined their farm, Harper noticed that one of the chicks wasn't a hen like they had thought. It was a rooster—a nice rooster that they named Jeremy. But as Jeremy, the other chickens, and the cats all got bigger, Harper noticed that Jeremy didn't like when the cats came to play.

Roosters are protective of hens, and even though Jeremy had grown up with the barn cats, he decided that he didn't want them playing with the hens anymore.

Harper felt sad for the cats when Jeremy chased them away.

"We don't peck at our friends!" she would yell to the rooster.

But Jeremy didn't listen. He just kept chasing the cats.

"It's hard when your friends won't play with you," Harper told the cats when they ran to her. "Maybe it's time to start hanging out with some other friends."

Harper walked over to Chunky. He was her favorite pony at the farm.

"Chunky will be your friend," she said to the cats.

The pony lowered his light-brown head. He sniffed the cats with his big nostrils, then let out a loud sigh. The four cats rubbed their heads against his legs and meowed.

Harper felt happy that the cats had a new friend.

And she also felt a little more ready to meet some new friends of her own.

PAWS AND PONDER

Have you ever had a friend stop talking to you like Harper did? How did that make you feel?

What makes someone a good friend?

How can you be a good friend to someone today?

Paws and Pray

Dear God, please help me to be a good friend. Help me share your love and kindness with others, and help me treat others like I want them to treat me. Thank you for loving me and for being my God and my friend.

Hay, Honor

Enthusiasm without knowledge is no good;
haste makes mistakes.

PROVERBS 19:2

HONOR, a German shepherd puppy, thought everything on the farm where he lived was for him.

He thought shoes, water bottles, and buckets were his toys.

He thought flower beds, sofa cushions, and mulch piles were places for him to sleep.

And he thought people's sandwiches and plates of cookies and all the other animals' food was for him to eat.

"That's not for you, Honor," his human mom, Jodi, said—a lot.

After a little while, Honor started to learn what was and wasn't his. Except for the horses' hay!

Every time Jodi fed her horses, Honor got so excited that he grabbed a mouthful of hay for himself.

The only trouble was, Honor didn't like the way hay tasted. So as soon as he pulled a clump of hay into his mouth, he ran to Jodi so she could take it out.

"Oh, Honor, you are so silly," Jodi said as she pulled pieces of hay off her puppy's tongue. "This hay is not for you."

But whenever Jodi pushed the wheelbarrow of hay to the next field, Honor forgot he didn't like hay, and he pulled a clump into his mouth again.

He looked at Jodi, tilted his head to the side, and tried to spit it out.

"When are you going to learn that this hay isn't for you, Honor?" Jodi laughed as she pulled more hay out of her puppy's mouth.

Honor watched the horses and donkeys eat the hay. He watched their teeth grind and chew it. Honor licked his lips.

"You're not going to like it," Jodi warned, knowing what her puppy was going to do.

And sure enough, Honor got so excited watching his horse friends eat that he picked a clump of hay off the ground yet again and started to chew.

Then he ran to Jodi—as usual—and opened his mouth so she could take out the yucky hay.

"Oh, Honor, when are you going to learn?"

PAWS AND PONDER

Why do you think Honor kept trying to eat the hay?

What is something that makes you really excited? Do you ever make mistakes when you get excited?

How can you remind yourself to slow down and make good choices?

Paws and Pray

Dear God, please help me make good choices and wise decisions. Help me remember to slow down and think before I do something. Thank you for giving me people who can help me learn what is right and wrong. And thank you for loving me, even when I mess up.

Teaching Indy

Listen to advice and accept instruction,
that you may gain wisdom in the future.

PROVERBS 19:20, ESV

GRACIE HAD A LOT TO LEARN when she was a puppy.

She had to learn to be gentle when she played with her family. She had to learn that not everything that fit in her mouth was food. And she had to learn to stay close to her family when they were outside.

Gracie loved chasing squirrels and following new smells, but one time, she chased a squirrel into the road and almost got hit by a car. Her family kept her on a leash for a long time after that, and they trained her to stay far back from the road. It took a while for Gracie to learn, but she did. And she never ran into the road again.

When Gracie was four years old, her next-door neighbors got a new puppy named Indy.

Gracie loved visiting Indy. He ran fast, he liked to play chase, and he shared his toys with her. Gracie and Indy became best friends and jumped and barked and wagged their tails whenever they saw each other.

One day when they were playing in the backyard, Indy noticed that the gate was open, and he ran right through it. He zoomed around the front yard in big circles, getting closer and closer to the road each time he ran. Indy's and Gracie's families yelled for him to come back. They tried to catch him, but he was too fast. Gracie could tell everyone was worried. She looked at Indy. She looked at her family. She looked at the road.

Then Gracie started running in circles around Indy. She kept getting closer to him, which moved him closer to his family. Finally, Indy's dad was able to grab him.

"Thank you, Gracie," he said, bending to pet her.

Gracie's tongue hung far out of her mouth. She was tired, but her wagging tail showed that she was also happy her friend was safe.

Indy is still a puppy who has a lot to learn. But with a family that loves him and a best friend who helps teach him, Indy will grow up to be a wise and happy dog.

PAWS AND PONDER

Why is it important for Indy to listen and learn from Gracie and his family?

What might happen if Indy doesn't listen and learn?

Who can you listen to and learn from? What is something that person has taught you?

Paws and Pray

Dear God, thank you for the people you've put in my life who help me learn. Help me listen to them, and help me obey you so I can grow in wisdom.

Mia's Lollipop

Many will say they are loyal friends,
but who can find one who is truly reliable?

PROVERBS 20:6

MIA DIDN'T LIKE when her parents argued—which they did a lot. It made her stomach hurt and her hands get cold. And it made her want to run away. She loved her parents. She just wished they loved each other.

Mia thought moving out of their small house and into a big new house would help things get better. But it had been a month, and her parents were arguing more than ever.

One day, Mia went outside to play and saw a sign across the street that said, "Free Kittens."

Mia squealed and ran back in the house.

"Mom, can I please, please get a kitty?" she begged. She promised she would take care of it.

Her mom smiled with her mouth, but her eyes still looked sad. "You may get a kitten, but you have to keep it on the back porch. I'm allergic to cat hair and can't have it inside."

Mia jumped up and hugged her mom. "Thanks, Mom! I will!"

Mia and her mom walked across the street to look at the three-month-old kittens. There were four left. Two were orange and white, one was gray, and one was black with white paws and a white neck.

Mia held and played with each one before choosing the cuddly orange one.

"She's sweet as a lollipop," the neighbor said, handing the kitten to Mia.

Mia thought Lollipop was a great name for her kitty. "I'll call you Lolly."

Mia took Lolly across the street to their screened-in porch. Mia put an old cushion down for Lolly's bed, set out two bowls for food and water, and asked her dad to buy kitten food from the store. Mia tied a long piece of yarn to a stick and laughed when Lolly started chasing the yarn.

"I love you, Lolly," Mia told her kitten.

And Lolly loved Mia back. The two played together every morning before school and every afternoon when Mia got home. When Lolly got bigger, Mia started taking her outside to play. And when Mia's parents argued, Mia scooped Lolly into her arms and sat with her under the big weeping willow tree in their backyard.

"I wish they wouldn't fight," Mia cried to Lolly one day, about a year after they had moved into their new house.

Mia's tears landed on Lolly's orange fur. The cat sat in Mia's lap and purred. Mia liked listening to Lolly purr. The sound made her feel safe and loved.

A few months later, when Mia's parents told her they were getting a divorce, Mia was really thankful Lolly was there to help her feel safe and loved. Mia knew everything was about to change, and she was scared and sad. But she also knew Lolly would be there with her, and she knew God would be with her too.

PAWS AND PONDER

What do you think Mia might have learned about God from Lolly?

Have you ever had something hard happen to you like Mia did? Who helped you through it?

What did you learn about God during that time?

Paws and Pray

Dear God, thank you for being my friend and for never leaving me. Help me to remember that I can talk to you anytime about anything.

Snow Deer

Ears to hear and eyes to see—
both are gifts from the LORD.

PROVERBS 20:12

SYDNEY HAD ALWAYS felt different.

Her brothers and sisters were tall. She was short.

Her friends never studied and got all As. She studied all the time and got Cs.

Her parents loved playing sports. She loved drawing pictures.

"Why am I so different?" Sydney wrote in her journal one night.

When she got up to close her curtains, she saw something strange in her backyard.

It was a white deer.

Sydney had heard some of their neighbors talk about a white deer that visited the neighborhood, but she had never actually seen it. Until now.

She had to squint to see all the brown deer standing nearby since they blended into the darkening woods behind her house. But not the white deer.

It was easy to see her.

"You don't fit in either, do you?" Sydney said, her face pressed against the window.

The deer pulled a few leaves off a bush, then walked away.

Sydney went to bed that night wondering if the deer knew how different she looked from the rest of her deer friends.

Sydney didn't see the white deer again for a long time.

But then, one cold winter's day, Sydney woke up to eight inches of snow. Her backyard looked like the North Pole. Her brothers and sisters were scurrying around trying to get dressed so they could go outside to play, but Sydney didn't feel like going outside. She wanted to sip hot chocolate and watch the snow fall from inside the warm house.

"You're so weird," her brother said.

His words hurt her feelings, but she pretended not to care.

As her brothers and sisters ran out the front door, she walked to the back window. Four brown deer—who must have gotten scared off by her brothers and sisters—ran through the backyard. Sydney had just taken a sip of her hot chocolate when the white deer walked into the yard.

At first it was hard to see her because she blended in so well. And when she stood still, it looked like someone had made a deer snowman. But then the deer moved. She looked majestic, like something from a fairy tale.

"You're beautiful," Sydney whispered.

Standing in the snow, the white deer didn't look out of place anymore. She looked like she was right where she belonged.

And maybe I am too, Sydney thought.

PAWS AND PONDER

Why did Sydney feel different from her friends and family?

Why did she feel better after seeing the white deer in the snow?

What do you like best about the way God made you?

Paws and Pray

Dear God, thank you for making me the way you did. On days when I feel different from everybody around me, or wish that I could be like someone else, please help me remember that you made me and that you love me just the way I am.

Lili's Animal Friends

The glory of the young is their strength; the gray hair of experience is the splendor of the old.

PROVERBS 20:29

LILI WAS ONLY FOUR when her mom and dad brought their little dog, Bella, home.

Lili had changed a lot in the eleven years since they got Bella, but Bella hadn't really changed that much. She was still a very small dog who only weighed five pounds.

A lot of people who saw Bella thought she was still a puppy. But Lili could tell Bella was different now.

Her little dog didn't play as much as she used to, she'd lost a lot of teeth, her fur had more gray in it, and she couldn't see very well.

Lili loved Bella, and she always would, but sometimes she wished she had a pet she could play with.

So when Lili found out that her friend's cat had

a litter of kittens, she asked her mom and dad if she could get one.

"I'll do all the work and keep the litter box in my room and clean it and everything," Lili said.

Lili was so happy when her parents said yes!

She used her own money to buy cat toys, a scratching post, and a little cat bed for the tan, black, and white kitten she named Miko.

When Miko first came home, he was smaller than Bella—but Miko grew fast! Soon the kitten was bigger than the dog. Miko didn't care about who was bigger and who was smaller. He just wanted to play!

But Bella did not.

Every time Miko pawed at Bella, jumped on her, or tried to sneak onto her bed, Bella growled and barked at him. Bella didn't want to play with a kitten. She wanted to sleep on her bed.

"Sorry, Bella. Someday he will learn you don't want to play," Lili told her dog.

Lili played with Miko as much as she could, but Miko wanted to wrestle and play-bite and swat with his paws—and since Lili didn't have a thick coat of fur like a cat or a dog, that kind of play left scratches on her skin.

"I think Miko needs a friend who will play with him," Lili told her parents after Miko had been with them for a few months.

She was surprised—and very happy—when they agreed with her.

A few weeks later, they brought home Mochi—a tan-and-black cat with a tiny white patch of fur under his chin. He was a month younger than Miko, and the two became best friends. They wrestled. They chased each other. They played hide-and-seek. And they snuggled together for naps.

Sometimes when Miko and Mochi lay in a sunny spot, Bella scooted in between them to take a short nap.

Thankfully, the cats finally learned not to wrestle with Bella.

And Bella learned that two kittens were really fun to watch.

PAWS AND PONDER

Why didn't Bella want to play with Miko?

In what ways were Miko and Mochi different from Bella? What is something Bella and the cats liked to do together?

What are some ways you are different from your grandparents? What are some things you like to do with them?

Paws and Pray

Dear God, thank you for making all different kinds of people and animals. Please help me to learn from people who are older and wiser than me. And please show me how to help others with the things I can do.

Where's Pluto?

Good planning and hard work lead to prosperity,
but hasty shortcuts lead to poverty.

PROVERBS 21:5

JOHN HAD A PET GECKO named Pluto. He liked carrying Pluto in his hand. Sometimes he even carried him in his pocket. John liked watching Pluto use his long tongue to catch bugs. And he liked how Pluto could burrow under almost anything.

But there was one thing John did not like about having a gecko: cleaning his tank.

Once a month, John had to clean the ten-gallon glass tank Pluto lived in. He always tried to put the job off as long as possible.

It wasn't a hard job. It just wasn't a *fun* job.

John had to put Pluto in a smaller plastic tank. Then he had to take everything out of the big glass tank—Pluto's basking rock, his food and water dishes, his climbing vine, and the little cave he slept in. He had to wash everything with hot water and a sponge, even the very dirty bottom of the tank.

"This is so gross and boring," John would mumble while he cleaned the tank in the downstairs bathroom. "I just want to go play."

One day, when John was in the middle of cleaning Pluto's tank, he ran upstairs to make sure his new game was downloading. When he turned to run, he didn't realize that his leg bumped the little plastic tank on the floor that Pluto was in and knocked the top off.

Thirty minutes later, after John's dad found him playing his game and sent him back downstairs, John realized Pluto was gone.

"Oh no! Where's Pluto?"

John looked everywhere—in the bathroom, under the table, inside the cabinets, even between the sofa cushions.

But there was no sign of Pluto.

John told his parents what had happened. They helped John look, but they couldn't find Pluto. John searched for hours, but there was no sign of his black-and-white gecko.

John's eyes got teary. He never meant for this to happen. He didn't mean to lose his friend. He had just wanted to play his game.

"Please come back, Pluto," John said that night as he crawled into bed.

"Please come back," he said the next morning while he ate his cereal.

"Please come back," he said after school when he started the search over again.

Two weeks after losing Pluto—thinking he would never see him again—John walked into the laundry room to look for his baseball socks. And guess who was hiding under his sock?

Pluto!

John picked up his gecko and ran to tell his parents. They all celebrated Pluto's return. Then John gently placed Pluto on his basking rock and closed the lid of the tank—tight.

"I'm so glad I found you," John said. "You are a lot of work, but you're worth it."

PAWS AND PONDER

Why didn't John like cleaning Pluto's tank?

Why was it important for him to work hard at his job even though he didn't like it?

What's a job or chore you don't like doing? Why is that job important for you to do?

Paws and Pray

Dear God, sometimes it's hard to do the things I'm responsible for. Please help me to remember that working hard and doing what I'm supposed to do is one way I can worship you. Help me want to do my best for you.

A Blue Slip for Pixie

Watch your tongue and keep your mouth shut, and you will stay out of trouble.

PROVERBS 21:23

"LET THE TEACHER TALK more than you today," Adelaide's dad told her as they pulled into the car line.

Adelaide put on her backpack and promised she would try. And she did. She really did. But when her teacher asked if anyone in the class had ever been skiing, Adelaide just had to tell her all about her family's ski trip last year—and about the car ride there, how scary the chairlift was, how her brother's head got stuck in the snow, and . . .

"Thank you for sharing, Adelaide," Mrs. Gardner interrupted. "That sounds like it was quite an adventure. Does anyone else have a story?"

Four other hands went up in the air. But Adelaide still had more to say. She started talking really fast.

"Adelaide," Mrs. Gardner said in her serious voice, "it's time to close your mouth and let someone else talk."

Ugh. Adelaide didn't want to close her mouth. She wanted to talk. But she didn't want to take home another blue slip to get signed by her parents. If she got another one, she would have to stay after school to help clean the classroom.

When Adelaide got home from school, her brown-and-white dog, Pixie, came running to greet her. Adelaide loved Pixie—especially because her dog never told her to close her mouth or to stop talking.

"Hi, Pixie!" Adelaide said. "Whatcha got?"

Pixie was holding one of Adelaide's toys in her mouth.

"No, no," Adelaide said, taking her toy away from the dog. "My toys are not your chew toys."

Adelaide threw a ball for Pixie and cheered when she caught it in the air.

"See, that's your toy," she said.

Later that evening, Pixie ran into the family room with one of Adelaide's stuffed animals in her mouth.

"Ugh, Pixie, my stuffed animals are supposed to stay in my room, not in your mouth!"

The next day, Adelaide came home with a blue slip.

She hadn't meant to talk more than the teacher, but they were doing an art project, and she got to sit by her best friend, Margo. Adelaide had so much to tell Margo! But Mrs. Gardner said her talking was making it hard for the rest of the class to do their work.

When Adelaide put the blue slip on the counter, she saw her favorite stuffed animal lying there—with a hole in its back and stuffing coming out.

"Pixie!" Adelaide yelled.

The brown-and-white dog walked into the kitchen—holding another one of Adelaide's toys in her mouth.

"I guess we both have to learn when to keep our mouths shut, don't we?" she said, patting her dog's head.

When Adelaide's mom came downstairs, she found two blue slips—one for Adelaide, and one that Adelaide had made for Pixie.

PAWS AND PONDER

What does it mean to "watch your tongue"?

Is it hard for you to keep your mouth closed sometimes?

How can we know when we should talk and when we should be quiet?

Paws and Pray

Dear God, please help me know what to say, when to say it, and when to keep my mouth shut. I want to use my words to help people and to show them your love. Please help me have self-control and wisdom so I can use my mouth and my words for you.

Tyler's Chicken

A good name is more desirable than great riches;
to be esteemed is better than silver or gold.

PROVERBS 22:1, NIV

TYLER LIKED GOING to his grandma's house. She was nice and fun and made good food. And she had a big yard and lots of animals.

Tyler's brother really liked playing with the dogs.

His sister liked playing with the bunnies.

They all liked watching the horses and feeding the goats.

But Tyler's favorite animals to visit were the chickens. He liked watching them peck at the ground, dig in the dirt, and flap their wings. And he really liked collecting their eggs with his grandma.

One day, while Tyler and his grandma were gathering the eggs inside the coop, Tyler heard a strange, loud clucking-yelling sound outside. He and

his grandma left the basket of eggs in the coop and went to see what was making the noise. It was a chicken named Charlotte. Four other chickens were pecking at her and chasing her. Tyler's grandma shooed the chickens away.

"Poor Charlotte keeps getting bullied by the other chickens," she said.

Tyler was surprised when his grandma picked Charlotte up and took her out of the chicken pen. Tyler grabbed the basket of eggs and joined his grandma outside the fence.

"I'm going to let her stay with me today," his grandma said.

She set Charlotte on the ground. Tyler thought the chicken would run away, but she didn't. She stayed close to his grandma and followed her while she did chores. Charlotte followed Grandma to the pasture to feed the horses. She followed her to the goat pen to feed the goats. She even ate some of the goats' food!

When it was time for lunch, Charlotte followed Tyler and his grandma to the house.

"Charlotte, you need to stay out here while we go have lunch," his grandma said.

Tyler asked if he could stay with Charlotte. He didn't want her to be lonely.

While Grandma made sandwiches inside, Tyler sat

on the grass and watched Charlotte peck the ground for bugs.

"You're a good chicken," Tyler told her.

Tyler was surprised when Charlotte walked over and sat on his lap! At first he felt a little nervous, but when Charlotte made a contented little clucking sound and closed her eyes, Tyler felt happy. He played with her for the rest of the day.

Every time Tyler visits his grandma's farm, he can't wait to see Charlotte. She knows his voice and comes running to him when he calls.

Tyler plays chase with her, he talks to her, and he always lets her sit on his lap.

Tyler thinks Charlotte is the most special chicken in the whole wide world. And every time she runs to him when he calls, Charlotte makes Tyler feel pretty special too.

PAWS AND PONDER

Why did Tyler's grandma take Charlotte out of the chicken coop?

How does Charlotte make Tyler feel special?

Think of someone who makes you feel special. How do you feel when you hear their name?

How do you feel when you hear God's name?

Paws and Pray

Dear God, you have the best name of all and deserve all my respect. Please help me live my life in a way that shows other people how good and kind you are.

Dolly and Apple Jack

Rich and poor have this in common:
The LORD is the Maker of them all.

PROVERBS 22:2, NIV

ANA SOFIA HAS always loved horses. Her bed is full of horse stuffed animals. Her notebooks are covered with pictures and drawings of horses. And most nights she dreams of horses. Since Ana Sofia's family owns a boarding stable—a place where people can pay to keep their horses—she doesn't just have to dream about them. Ana Sofia gets to see horses every day.

She gets to help take care of large draft horses with fuzzy feet, pretty paint horses with blue eyes, strong racehorses with fast legs, and small ponies with big personalities. Ana Sofia thinks each one is special and beautiful, and she likes visiting with them all.

But she has two favorites: Dolly and Apple Jack. These two horse friends couldn't be more different.

Dolly is a beautiful show horse. She competes in dressage, which Ana Sofia says is like a dance competition for horses. Dolly's owners spend hours and hours each week training with her. Before competitions, they spend hours and hours washing her dark-brown coat, brushing her, and putting ribbons through her black mane and special wrappings on her legs. Dolly has won many competitions and has made a lot of money for her owners.

Apple Jack is a small pony who was rescued by a kind woman. The woman heard about the abandoned pony in need of a home and spent her own money to bring him to the boarding stable owned by Ana Sofia's family. The woman didn't know much about horses, but she wanted to save Apple Jack. Apple Jack's light-brown coat and blond mane are usually covered in dirt and reddish-orange mud. Apple Jack will never win any competitions, but—like Dolly—he is one of the nicest, gentlest horses Ana Sofia has ever known.

Dolly and Apple Jack are so different, but they are friends. And they both make Ana Sofia feel happy when she is with them. Dolly doesn't know—or care—that she is a superstar at the stable. Apple Jack doesn't mind that he's usually covered in mud, and he never feels jealous of all of Dolly's fancy ribbons. They are just happy to be together—eating grass, running in open pastures, and sniffing Ana Sofia's pockets to find the treats she always brings them.

Dolly and Apple Jack may look different and do different things, but Ana Sofia knows that when they look at each other, they just see their friends. Friends who like being together—and searching Ana Sofia's pockets.

PAWS AND PONDER

What do you think Dolly and Apple Jack have taught Ana Sofia about friendship?

Do you ever feel jealous of your friends? How can you remind yourself to be thankful for what you do have when you start to feel jealous of someone?

What are you thankful for today?

Paws and Pray

Dear God, thank you for my family, my home, the food I have to eat, my friends—and most of all, for your love. When I start to feel jealous of others, please remind me of everything I have. And help me to share what I have with others.

What Was That?

The prudent see danger and take refuge,
but the simple keep going and pay the penalty.

PROVERBS 22:3, NIV

ZURI'S MOUTH OPENED in a huge yawn. She was excited to watch a lunar eclipse with her family, but it was almost midnight and she was getting really tired.

She snuggled under the thick blanket her mom had brought outside. Zuri, her mom, her brother Darius, and their dog Lucy were lying on the back deck to watch the moon pass through Earth's shadow.

"Look! It's starting!" Darius shouted.

It looked like God had drawn a dark, reddish-brown line on the left side of the moon. And as she watched, the line got wider and wider until half of the moon was reddish-brown. Zuri didn't feel sleepy anymore. The show in the sky was way too exciting.

As Zuri snuggled farther under the covers, Lucy jumped up and started growling. It was a low rumbling sound that Zuri had never heard her dog make before.

Zuri, Darius, and their mom stared into the backyard, but it was too dark for them to see anything. Lucy growled again.

HAAA-OOOO!

Goose bumps rose on Zuri's arms at the scary howling sound. Whatever made that sound was close. Too close.

"What was that?" she whispered.

"A coyote," Darius and her mom said at the same time.

Zuri had never seen a coyote in real life before, but she knew they could be dangerous. Lucy growled again, and Zuri felt even more scared.

What if Lucy tries to chase the coyote like she chases deer and squirrels? A coyote probably wouldn't run away like a squirrel or deer. Zuri's heart started to beat fast.

The hair on Lucy's neck stood straight up. Her whole body looked ready to run. But she didn't. She just stood there growling.

"Time for us to go in," Zuri's mom said.

Zuri looked up at the moon. It was almost totally covered in the red-brown shadow. But she didn't care about the lunar eclipse anymore. She just wanted Lucy—and her family—to be safe.

Her mom held on to Lucy's collar as they walked inside. But Lucy didn't even try to run off the deck. She seemed to know that it was better to follow her family inside.

Zuri was a little sad they didn't get to see the entire eclipse, but she was happy to be secure inside with her family. And she was even happier when her mom let her eat ice cream at midnight!

PAWS AND PONDER

How did Lucy react to the danger of the coyote?

What might have happened if she had run after the coyote?

Zuri and her family took refuge in their house. What are some other safe places—or safe people—you can go to when things feel scary?

Paws and Pray

Dear God, thank you for giving me safe places and safe people I can turn to when I am scared. Help me to be a safe place for others. And help me to remember to run to you when I'm afraid.

Finding Delta

Train up a child in the way he should go;
even when he is old he will not depart from it.

PROVERBS 22:6, ESV

GUNNER, a golden retriever puppy, bounced up and down like Tigger from Winnie-the-Pooh. He was excited because his human mom, Marie, was taking him to work with her at the Dolphin Research Center. She was a dolphin trainer—Gunner didn't know what that meant, but he knew it must mean something good because his mom always came home smelling like salt water, fish, and other animals.

After Gunner sniffed some of Marie's friends at the center, she said it was time to go to the water.

Water was one of Gunner's favorite words!

Gunner tugged on his leash to get Marie to walk faster.

"Hold on, bud," Marie laughed. "You don't know where we're going yet. Watch."

Gunner knew the word *watch*, too. It meant he was supposed to look up at Marie and follow her. So he did. Gunner followed Marie down a winding path, past a tall cage with birds inside, to a lagoon where Gunner saw two brown animals playing with a ball in the water. Marie said they were called sea lions. Then they walked down a wooden dock and through a gate to another dock.

Gunner was excited because they were so close to the water. Was Marie going to let him swim? Gunner's body started to wiggle back and forth. He could almost feel the water on his fur.

SPLASH!

The strangest-looking animal Gunner had ever seen stared up at him. It looked like a giant fish.

"Gunner, this is Delta the dolphin," Marie said. "Delta wants to say hi."

Marie raised her hand in the air and blew a whistle, and Delta waved his paw—which Marie called a flipper.

Gunner lay on his belly and stretched his head as far as he could to sniff Delta. The dolphin popped out of the water and bumped Gunner's nose. Gunner jumped up and barked. Then he lay back down so Delta could do it again.

Gunner learned the way to Delta's lagoon, and every time Marie brought him to work, he wanted to go see Delta first. Gunner learned to drop toys in the water for Delta to bring back. And he really liked to bump noses with his dolphin friend.

The people who came to see the dolphins took lots of pictures of Gunner and Delta. They were even on the news a few times. But Gunner didn't care about any of that. He just liked to visit his dolphin friend.

Gunner is much older now and moves a lot slower than he did when he was a puppy. But whenever he goes to work with Marie, he still heads right to Delta's lagoon. He learned the way years ago, and he will never ever forget how to get back to his friend Delta.

PAWS AND PONDER

Why will Gunner never forget how to find Delta?

What is something you hope you never forget as you grow up?

What are some things you can do now to help you remember God and learn more about him as you get older?

Paws and Pray

Dear God, thank you for giving us the Bible and people who can teach us about you. Help me to never forget you. And when I make mistakes, help me to always find my way back to you.

Chores Are for the Birds

Blessed are those who are generous,
because they feed the poor.

PROVERBS 22:9

MAKS AND EVIE didn't want to do chores on a Saturday, especially when all their friends were having fun playing. And they really didn't want to have to wash their mom's car. Why did they have to clean the car when they couldn't even drive?

Their dad always washed the cars when he was home from his job with the military. But he had been gone for six months. And before he left, he had asked Maks and Evie to help out at home. They wanted to do what he asked. But doing chores was not fun.

Maks sprayed the car with water while Evie wiped it with a soapy rag. Birds chirped and sang in the distance, and when Maks turned his head to look at one, he accidentally sprayed Evie. She squealed and threw

the soapy rag at him. Suddenly, their boring chore turned into a fun game of water tag. After twenty minutes, their mom's car was clean, but both brother and sister were soaked, and a giant puddle had formed in the middle of the driveway.

As Maks and Evie put the hose and buckets away, birds started flying into the puddle. A red bird used it as a bathtub, two little brown birds drank from it, and a bluebird stood in the middle of the puddle and chirped. Maks and Evie watched the birds from the deck.

"It has been really dry recently," Evie said. "I bet the water feels good to them."

That gave Maks an idea.

"Let's give them lots of water spots," he suggested.

So Maks and Evie set up their old water table toy on the deck and filled it to the top. They filled four old shallow pots and lined them up on the deck rail. While Maks added more water to the driveway puddle, Evie found birdseed in the garage and refilled the old bird feeder on the deck. Then they went inside and waited for the birds to find what they had left out.

It didn't take long.

Two little reddish-brown birds landed on the water table. One dipped his head and wings in the water, while the other one drank. A blue-and-gray bird splashed back and forth in one of the shallow pots.

Three black-and-white birds played in the driveway puddle. And all of them took turns at the bird feeder.

It felt good to help the little birds—and their mom. So good, in fact, that Maks and Evie forgot all about not wanting to do chores on a Saturday.

PAWS AND PONDER

Why did Maks and Evie feel better after they helped the birds?

Why does God want us to be generous and help others?

What is something you can do to help another living creature today?

Paws and Pray

Dear God, sometimes it is hard to help other people, especially if it's boring or takes me away from something that feels more fun. Please help me want to serve others. Help me be generous with my time, finding ways to show your love to the people around me.

You Can Do It, Raven

I am teaching you today—yes, you—
so you will trust in the LORD.

PROVERBS 22:19

"YOU CAN DO IT, RAVEN," nine-year-old Annie called out to her dog from the lake.

"Don't be scared!" her six-year-old brother, Asher, added. "You can swim."

But Raven didn't believe them. She wanted to. She kept running into the water, splashing and wagging her fluffy black tail, but as soon as the water hit her belly, she turned and ran back to the shore.

Annie and Asher didn't like seeing Raven so scared—especially of something they knew their dog would like if she tried. So they decided to show Raven how to do the dog paddle.

"Watch us, Raven!" Asher yelled.

Annie and Asher bent their elbows and used their

hands like paddles to swim. Raven jumped up and down on the shore. She wanted to join them, but she was just too scared.

Annie and Asher's dad picked Raven up and carried her out into the lake. He planned to hold her until she felt safe enough to swim. But Raven had other ideas.

As soon as the water hit her belly, Raven started clawing her way up their dad's back until her front legs were on his head. She jumped from his shoulders into the shallow water and ran all the way back to the sandy shore.

Because their family liked to visit the lake near their house every summer, Annie and Asher really wanted Raven to learn to swim. But they worried she would never want to get in the water again.

A few days later, when they were all down at the lake, Raven met a dog named Lady. The two of them started running and jumping and playing together. Raven was so happy to have another dog to play with that she forgot about being scared of the water. When Lady ran into the water, Raven followed her. Annie and Asher stopped splashing to watch what would happen.

Raven stopped as soon as the cool water touched the fur on her belly, but Lady kept going. Lady started swimming once the water got deep enough. She turned her head to look for Raven and barked a high bark. It was like she was saying, *"Come on!"*

Raven looked at Lady.

She looked at Annie and Asher.

She looked back at the shore.

"You can do it, girl," Annie and Asher whispered, wishing they could give Raven some of their courage.

Raven barked.

She wagged her tail.

And then . . . she took four more steps into the lake and started dog-paddling after Lady.

Annie and Asher gave each other high fives and cheered for Raven.

But Raven didn't hear them. She was having too much fun swimming!

PAWS AND PONDER

Have you ever had to do something that felt scary? Did it feel as scary after you did it?

How can someone you trust help you when you are scared?

How does knowing you can trust God give you courage?

Paws and Pray

Dear God, sometimes I get too scared to do things—even good things. Please help me learn to trust you with scary things. And thank you for giving me people to encourage me.

Hi, Rosie

There is surely a future hope for you,
and your hope will not be cut off.

PROVERBS 23:18, NIV

TWO MONTHS AFTER Drew's dog Jade died, his mom told him to come downstairs because she and his dad had a surprise. When Drew got down to the living room, he saw his mom holding a puppy! The fuzzy, yellow dog was wiggling in her arms and trying to lick her face.

"What do you think of our new puppy?" his mom asked.

Drew jumped up and down. He couldn't remember ever feeling so happy.

"What should we name her?" his dad said.

His mom put the puppy on the floor. Before Drew could answer, the puppy ran over to the basket of

pretend flowers Drew's mom kept by the fireplace, pulled out a red rose, and started chewing it.

His mom tried to save the rose, but it was covered in tiny teeth marks.

"How about Rosie?" Drew laughed.

His parents laughed too. "Rosie is a great name," his dad agreed.

Drew loved having Rosie around. She did a lot of funny things. She climbed into flowerpots outside. She took dirty clothes from the laundry baskets and scattered them around the house. And she hid her toys inside Drew's dad's shoes.

But after a few weeks, Drew started getting frustrated with Rosie. She chewed up his shoes, knocked over his Lego set, and made a mess on the carpet in his room. And every time he put Rosie on his bed, she wanted to play tug-of-war with his sheets.

"I wish Jade were still here," Drew said, missing his other dog. "She never messed up my room."

"I know, buddy. I miss her too," his mom said. She picked up Rosie and held her. "Did you know that once when Jade was a puppy, she took all the stuffing out of my pillow? It looked like it had snowed inside the house."

Drew giggled. He couldn't imagine Jade doing something like that.

"And another time, she grabbed the end of a roll

of toilet paper and started running. There were toilet-paper streamers everywhere."

"Really?" Drew laughed.

"Really," his mom said. "Jade wasn't always the well-behaved dog you remember. But just like we helped Jade learn, we will help Rosie learn. And I'm sure she will grow up to be a very good dog too."

The next day, Drew went outside to play with Rosie. Jade had been so sick the last few years that she hadn't wanted to play. But Rosie loved to run and fetch. After an hour, Drew took Rosie back inside. They each had a long drink of water. Then Drew sat down on the floor to play a video game. He smiled when Rosie curled up beside him and fell right to sleep.

Drew rubbed her soft ears. "You're a good dog, Rosie, just like your big sister Jade was."

PAWS AND PONDER

Proverbs 23:18 talks about hope. What does it mean to have hope?

How did the stories Drew's mom told about Jade as a puppy give Drew hope?

What is something you are hoping for today?

Paws and Pray

Dear God, thank you for giving us hope even when things feel hopeless. I know I can have hope during hard times because you say in the Bible that you are always with me. Help me to trust you no matter what.

No, Greta

Do you like honey? Don't eat too much,
or it will make you sick!

PROVERBS 25:16

ANNA AND HER SIBLINGS love playing with their dog, Greta. They especially like running around their big backyard with her. It was good that Greta had a big yard because she was part Bernese mountain dog, and those large dogs are sometimes used to move sheep from one place to another.

It made Anna and her brother and sisters laugh when Greta tried to herd *them* like sheep! When Greta wasn't herding her family, she liked to go for walks, sit with them while they did homework, and snuggle with them at bedtime.

They all agreed that their black, white, and brown dog was just about perfect in every way—except one.

Greta had a bad habit that they couldn't get her to stop.

She ate paper towels.

And not just one or two. Greta wanted to eat every paper towel she could find!

She grabbed them from the trash, took them off the table, and sneaked them out of lunch boxes. It didn't matter if the paper towel was clean or dirty, wadded up or flat, or draped on someone's knee. Greta would take it and eat it!

At first Anna and her brother and sisters thought Greta's paper-towel snacks were funny. But one day when Greta got really sick after eating a bunch of paper towels, they realized there was nothing funny about her bad habit.

Greta got so sick that Anna's mom and dad had to take her to the animal hospital. They took some X-rays and found a giant wad of paper towels in her intestines. The vet said one or two paper towels in a dog her size wouldn't cause a problem, but a lot of them could be trouble.

Greta had to stay in the animal hospital for several days while the vet gave her medicine to get the paper towels unstuck. Thankfully, the medicine worked and Greta got to go home.

Anna hoped Greta had learned her lesson about paper towels. But a few days later, the dog was back to her old ways, rummaging through the trash for a paper-towel snack.

"No, Greta!" Anna yelled, running to take the paper towel away. "Those make you sick. Have a doggy treat instead."

Thankfully, Greta has a house full of people to help her learn that dog treats taste much better than paper towels—and that herding her human family is a lot more fun than going to the animal hospital.

PAWS AND PONDER

Have you ever eaten too much and gotten a stomachache?

What are some other things, besides food, that might make us feel bad—or are bad for us—if we have too much of them?

How can we be careful not to have too much of something, even if it's good?

Paws and Pray

Dear God, thank you for all the wonderful gifts you have given me. Please help me to make wise choices and to know when I've had too much of a good thing.

Ethan Wants to Quit

Singing cheerful songs to a person with a heavy heart is like taking someone's coat in cold weather or pouring vinegar in a wound.

PROVERBS 25:20

ETHAN WAS READY. All he had to do was kick the ball into the net and his team would win. He took a deep breath. He kicked with all his might. And . . . he missed.

The other team cheered.

Ethan's team groaned.

And Ethan wanted to run away.

Some of his teammates tried to be nice and said, "It's okay. You'll get it next time." Other teammates glared at him. His coach patted him on the back and said, "You'll make the next one."

His parents took him out for ice cream after the game. He knew they were trying to cheer him up, but

he just wanted to go home. His older sister tried to make him laugh by telling him silly jokes. But instead of making Ethan laugh, her jokes made him mad.

And when some kids from the other team showed up at the ice cream shop, laughing, high-fiving each other, and passing around their trophy, Ethan felt really, *really* mad.

Ethan threw his soccer uniform in the laundry basket when he got home and crawled under his covers. He kept remembering how it felt to stand in front of the net and miss the goal.

"I never want to play soccer again," he cried into his pillow.

Ethan's bedroom door opened. He closed his eyes and pretended to be asleep. He didn't want anyone to try making him feel better. He just wanted to be sad and mad for a little while.

But it wasn't his mom, or his dad, or his sister. It was his dog, Oreo.

Oreo jumped on Ethan's bed and snuggled close to him. Ethan put his arm around his dog's black-and-white neck. His dog sighed a deep sigh and laid his head beside Ethan's.

"I missed the kick," Ethan said.

Oreo scooted his head a little closer and closed his eyes. Ethan told Oreo how embarrassed he had felt, how mad he was at the other team—and himself—and how he never wanted to play soccer again.

Oreo rolled onto his side so Ethan could rub his belly. The more Ethan talked to Oreo, the better he started to feel. And when his mom and dad came to say good night, Ethan asked them if they would come to his next game.

"So you're not quitting?" his dad said, somehow knowing what Ethan had been thinking.

"No," Ethan answered. "Everyone misses a kick once in a while. I'll make the next one."

And he did.

PAWS AND PONDER

What made Ethan so mad? How did Oreo help him feel better?

What do you need when you are mad, sad, or embarrassed?

How can you help a friend or family member who is feeling that way?

Paws and Pray

Dear God, thank you for always listening to me, no matter how I feel. Please help me be a good friend to others when they're upset, even if that means listening more than I talk.

Poor Ruby

Too much honey is bad for you, and so
is trying to win too much praise.

PROVERBS 25:27, GNT

CALEB REALLY LIKES making his friends laugh. He tells jokes, acts silly, makes noises, and yells out in class so people will think he's funny. Caleb and his dog, Ruby, are a lot alike in that way. Except Ruby doesn't try to get people to laugh. She tries to get people to give her treats.

Ruby will do anything for a treat—even a tiny crumb of cake! She will sit, lie down, shake hands, roll over, beg, or drop a toy. Her love of treats made it easy to train her and teach her tricks. But when Caleb's little brother, Liam, had his fourth birthday party, Ruby's love of treats caused her to have a big stomachache.

Caleb and Liam's mom had decorated the kitchen and dining room with streamers, balloons, and "Happy

Birthday" signs. Ten of Liam's friends from preschool came to the party, and they all wanted to play with Ruby.

The brown hound dog loved the attention—*and* the treats she got for doing tricks!

"Watch!" Liam shouted to his friends while Caleb was in the kitchen helping his mom put away the left-overs. "Ruby can shake hands."

The kids all clapped and started telling Ruby to shake their hands. Caleb could tell every time Ruby shook someone's hand because they all clapped for her.

And they clapped a lot.

"Is everyone all done with their cake?" Caleb's mom asked, walking back into the dining room. "Oh my . . ."

Ruby's whiskers and nose were covered in blue and white icing. And it looked like she even had some icing on her ear.

"Look, Liam's mom! Ruby can shake my hand!" Liam's friend Jamal put his hand out for Ruby, then gave her a piece of birthday cake.

"Oh, Ruby, you just couldn't stop doing tricks, could you?" their mom asked.

Caleb helped his mom clean Ruby's face and ears. And later that night, he helped her clean up an even bigger mess when Ruby got sick from all the cake she ate.

Caleb was glad that making people laugh didn't cause him to get sick like Ruby. But it did cause him to have to stay after school sometimes—and if he really got in trouble, he couldn't play video games for a week.

"Maybe we both need to learn when it's time to stop," he told Ruby.

She looked up at him, and her stomach gurgled loudly. *Poor Ruby.*

PAWS AND PONDER

- Is it wrong for Caleb to want to make people laugh? When might his love of making people laugh become a problem?
- What are some other ways people try to earn too much praise?
- Why can trying to earn too much praise get us in trouble?

Paws and Pray

Dear God, thank you for loving me the way I am. Thank you that I don't have to earn your love, and thank you that I can't lose your love either. Help me want to please you more than anyone else.

Brave Penny

The heartfelt counsel of a friend is as sweet as perfume and incense.

PROVERBS 27:9

MILA WISHED it wasn't so hard for her to talk to people. Her best friend Summer could talk to anyone—other kids, parents, even teachers! But whenever Mila tried to talk to someone, other than her parents or her friends, her insides got shaky, her fingers tingled, and her head felt fuzzy.

"She's just a regular person," Summer said one day when Mila was scared to ask her teacher a question after school.

Mila knew her friend was mostly right. Mrs. Thompson *was* a person. But she wasn't a regular person. She was their teacher. And Mila wasn't so sure teachers were *regular* people.

She also wasn't sure that doctors, grocery store

workers, teenagers, or her parents' friends were regular people. Talking to them felt too scary for them to be regular people.

"I wish I could talk to people like I talk to you," Mila said to her betta fish Penny as she sprinkled fish food into her bowl.

Penny swam up to the top of the tank to eat. Mila laid her finger on the water and laughed when Penny bumped it.

Mila had won the little fish at the state fair two months earlier. At first, Penny had seemed scared of the big fishbowl that sat on the table by Mila's bed. She hid inside a pirate-ship decoration and wouldn't come out. But after a few days, Penny started swimming all around her tank.

Mila talked to Penny every night before she fell asleep. She told her all about her friends, what she was working on at school, what she wanted for her birthday, and how hard it was to talk to people.

"I have to talk to Mrs. Thompson tomorrow," Mila told Penny one night. "I was sick last week, so I have to ask her when I can make up my math test." Mila's stomach started to hurt just thinking about it. "I wish I could swim around a bowl all day like you do. Then I wouldn't have to talk to anybody."

Penny swam into her pirate ship. It made Mila

remember how scared the little fish had been the first day Mila brought her home.

"But you're not scared anymore," Mila said.

She touched the water with her index finger. Penny swam out of the pirate ship and bumped her finger. Mila closed her eyes and took a deep breath.

"If you can be brave, I can be brave too," she told the little fish.

The very next day, Mila walked up to her teacher's desk and asked when she should take her math test. Mrs. Thompson said she could take the test after lunch. Mila felt so brave! As she turned to go back to her seat, she noticed that Mrs. Thompson had a picture of a betta fish on her desk.

Maybe teachers really are regular people, Mila thought with a smile.

PAWS AND PONDER

Why do you think Mila was so scared to talk to people?

How did Penny help Mila feel brave?

What is something you feel scared to do?

Who can you talk to when you're scared?

Paws and Pray

Dear God, thank you for being close to me when I'm afraid. Thank you for giving me friends and animals who help me feel brave. Please show me how to help others be brave too.

Oscar's Growl

As a face is reflected in water, so the heart reflects the real person.

PROVERBS 27:19

JARED HADN'T MEANT to write a mean word on Connor's paper, or to tease Hannah at recess. He didn't know why he did those things to his friends. It was the third time Jared's teacher had sent a note home that week to get signed.

Jared shoved the note in his pocket as he stepped off the school bus. He just wanted to get inside his house and see his dog, Oscar.

"Oscar?" Jared called out.

He dropped his backpack on the floor and went searching for his black Lab. He looked in all of Oscar's favorite places: the sofa, his dog bed, the top of the stairs, in front of the refrigerator.

Jared finally found Oscar hiding under his bed.

He started to reach under the bed to pull Oscar out, but Oscar growled at him.

Oscar never growled, not even when Jared's baby cousin Gabe pulled his ears. Jared knew something must be wrong.

"Mom!" Jared called.

His mom came out of her upstairs office and helped get Oscar out from under Jared's bed. Oscar's eyes were droopy, and he was panting hard. He looked really sick, so they took him right to the vet.

"He has a serious infection under his skin," the animal doctor said to Jared's mom. "And he needs surgery to clean it out."

Jared didn't want Oscar to have surgery, but he didn't want his dog to be in pain either.

"The doctor will call us when the surgery is over," his mom said when they got home. She gave Jared a hug. "You were smart to realize that Oscar's growl meant he was hurting inside."

When his mom said that, Jared's stomach did a little flip, like it did when he rode the Tower of Terror at Disney World last year.

"Um, Mom?" he said. "I kind of growled at someone today too."

Jared handed her the note from school.

"I was mean to my friends because I got mad," he explained. "But I don't think I was really mad at *them*."

"Are you missing Grandma?" his mom asked.

Jared's throat started to burn. He nodded.

Jared's grandma had died two months ago. He used to see her every weekend, and he did miss her—a lot. She used to make him cookies, and she always listened to his stories. She even learned to play his favorite video game with him. His mom had tried to talk about his grandma with him, but Jared didn't want to make his mom sad—and he didn't want to feel sad either—so he always changed the subject.

Jared's mom sat beside him on his bed, and they talked about how much they missed Grandma. Talking about her was hard, but it also helped Jared feel a little better.

The vet called a few hours later. Oscar's surgery was over, and he could go home the next day. Jared was so happy to know Oscar was going to be okay.

"I'll say I'm sorry to Connor and Hannah tomorrow," he told his mom after she signed the note. "And next time I miss Grandma, I'll try not to growl at my friends."

PAWS AND PONDER

Why did Oscar growl?

Why was Jared mean to his friends?

Have you ever treated someone badly because you were hurting inside?

Who can you talk to about your feelings?

Paws and Pray

Dear God, sometimes I have really big feelings, and I don't know what to do with them. Help me remember that I can talk to you about all my feelings. Help me to be brave and go to a person I trust when I am hurting inside. Please show me how I can help someone who might be hurting today.

Little Thief

Whoever conceals his transgressions will not prosper,
but he who confesses and forsakes them will obtain mercy.

PROVERBS 28:13, ESV

THUD!

"What was that noise?" Kiley asked.

"It sounded like a buffalo fell down," her older brother, Alex, answered.

A few minutes later, their big three-year-old dog, Honey, ran down the stairs. She looked guilty as she walked into the family room with her head down. When she stopped, her big brown eyes looked up at Kiley.

"Hey!" Kiley yelled. "You little thief. That's my teddy bear!"

Suddenly, the loud noise they had heard a few minutes ago made sense.

Honey must have jumped up onto Kiley's bed, taken

her teddy bear, and jumped back down. Thankfully, she had brought the bear to Kiley instead of hiding and ripping the stuffing out like she did when she was a puppy.

Kiley took her bear out of Honey's mouth and wiped off the slobber.

"You play with *your* toys, Honey," Kiley said.

And she did. For a while.

But a few days later, Kiley and Alex heard another *THUD*.

Honey came running down the stairs. She looked guilty as she walked into the family room with her head down. Her big brown eyes looked up at Alex.

"Hey!" Alex shouted. "You little thief. Those are my socks!"

Kiley giggled at the sight of Honey holding her brother's smelly socks in her mouth.

Alex took his socks away from Honey. "My socks aren't your toys," he told the dog. "Play with your toys."

Honey obeyed. For a while.

But a few weeks later, Kiley and Alex were watching a movie with their parents when they all heard a loud *THUD*.

Honey came running down the stairs. She walked into the family room looking guilty with her head down. This time, her big brown eyes looked up at Kiley and Alex's mom.

"Hey!" their mom said. "You little thief. That book was on my bed!"

Kiley and Alex laughed.

Their dog may have been a little thief, but at least she always brought things back.

PAWS AND PONDER

How did Honey's family react when she took something that wasn't hers?

What do you do after you've done something wrong? Do you admit the truth to someone you trust, or do you try to hide?

Do you need to ask God to forgive you for something today?

Paws and Pray

Dear God, please forgive me for trying to hide the wrong things I do from you. Help me to remember that you'll forgive me when I confess my sins. And help me to obey and trust you.

Learning to Trust

The fear of man lays a snare,
but whoever trusts in the LORD is safe.

PROVERBS 29:25, ESV

KAYSIE WAS FIVE YEARS OLD when she was adopted from an orphanage in China. She was happy to have a family and a new home, but she was scared of a lot of things back then. Her new family felt like strangers, she couldn't understand what anyone was saying, and because of severe damage to her left leg when she was little, she had to have a big surgery to remove the lower part of her leg.

Being in a strange place with new people—and having to learn how to walk on a prosthetic leg—was really hard. But Kaysie's family loved her, and they helped her through those hard days.

Over time, Kaysie figured out how to walk on her new leg, and she learned how to talk with her new

family. But just as Kaysie was feeling better about everything, she fell and broke her arm.

Kaysie had to go back to the hospital to get her arm fixed. While she was there, she met a big, white, friendly looking dog. The woman holding the dog's leash said he was a therapy dog and asked if he could say hi. Kaysie nodded, then laughed when the dog put his paws up on her bed. Kaysie buried her face in his thick fur. Her heart felt warm and happy.

"I want to have a dog like you someday," she whispered.

Even after Kaysie went home and her arm healed, she kept thinking about the therapy dog. She asked her parents if she could get a dog of her own and train him to be a therapy dog. Her parents thought it was a good idea. They suggested training the dog to help her with things too.

"You could teach the dog to help you keep your balance when you go downstairs," they suggested.

Kaysie loved that idea. She could do most things that people with two complete legs could do, but some things *were* harder, and it would be nice to have a helper.

Soon, Kaysie was meeting her very own dog, an Australian shepherd puppy she named Rusty.

Kaysie remembered how scared she was when she joined a new family. She spent a lot of time with Rusty so he could get to know her. She also taught him lots of words, commands, and tricks so she could communicate with him.

One trick Kaysie loved to do with Rusty was a trust fall. She taught him to sit on his back legs and fall backward into her arms. The trick took a lot of trust for Rusty, but Rusty learned that Kaysie would never let him fall.

Rusty was still a puppy, but he was already learning how to be a therapy and helper dog. He and Kaysie started working with a therapy dog group called Canines for Christ.

Kaysie hopes people will feel God's love when they visit with her and Rusty. And she also hopes that when they see Rusty do his trust-fall trick, they will learn that they can trust God as much as she and Rusty trust each other.

PAWS AND PONDER

What were some things Kaysie had to learn when she came to live with her family?

How did she help Rusty learn to trust her?

How might Rusty's trust-fall trick help people learn that they can trust God?

What is something you need to trust God with today?

Paws and Pray

Dear God, help me remember that I can trust you with everything. Thank you for being so trustworthy. Please help me find ways to show others your love.

Hemingway's Promise

Every word of God proves true.
He is a shield to all who come to him for protection.

PROVERBS 30:5

ELLA LOOKED UP at the big house her mom wanted to visit during their vacation to the Florida Keys.

"Whose house is this again?" she asked.

"A famous author named Ernest Hemingway," her older brother, Andrew, answered. "He lived here with his wife Pauline from 1931 to 1939."

Ella knew her brother was smart, but how did he know *that*?

When Ella spun around to ask him, she saw that he was reading from a sign near the ticket booth.

"Cheater," she teased.

He shrugged his shoulders and laughed.

Ella laughed too, but then her heart did a little flop

and she felt sad. She was going to miss her brother when he left for college next month. She had been so excited to take this big trip with her family to celebrate his high school graduation, but each day that passed meant her big brother was one day closer to leaving.

Most of her friends talked about how much they didn't like their siblings. But Ella loved spending time with Andrew. He was her best friend.

What if everything changes when he goes to college? She worried.

It was their turn to go into the two-story white house with yellow shutters. It looked old and important. But as soon as Ella saw a cat lying in the middle of a room, nothing else mattered.

"Andrew!" she squealed. "This cat has six toes on her paws!"

Andrew knelt down beside his sister and pulled out his phone to take a picture. A lady with a name tag walked over and started telling them about Hemingway's cats.

"They are polydactyl cats," she explained. "That means they have extra toes."

She explained how Mr. Hemingway got a six-toed cat as a gift from a ship captain. The woman said that Hemingway's cats became like family, and he promised to always take care of them—which he did until he died. Today, she said, his house was a museum, and

the cats were being taken care of by the people who worked there. And there were a *lot* of cats to take care of! But they all looked happy and healthy.

Ella was glad Hemingway kept his promise to his cats. It reminded her of how God keeps his promise to take care of his children.

Ella and Andrew took a picture of every cat they found.

"Andrew?" she asked while they waited for their parents in the gift shop. "Will you still want to hang out with me when you go to college?"

Andrew stopped petting the orange cat by his feet and looked at Ella.

"I'll always want to hang out with you. You're my little buddy—and you always will be."

Ella was still going to miss her brother, but she felt a lot better. After all, if Hemingway could keep his promise to his cats, she knew that, with God's help, she and Andrew could keep their promises to each other.

PAWS AND PONDER

Why was Ella worried that everything might change when her brother went to college?

What did her brother say that made her feel much better?

Can you think of any promises God has made? If not, ask a trusted adult to help you find one in the Bible.

Paws and Pray

Dear God, thank you for always keeping your promises. I know that I can trust you and that you will never let me down.

About the Author

JENNIFER MARSHALL BLEAKLEY is also the author of *Joey: How a Blind Rescue Horse Helped Others Learn to See* and *Project Solomon: The True Story of a Lonely Horse Who Found a Home—and Became a Hero,* as well as the Pawverbs devotional series. She has worked as a child and family grief counselor and holds a master's degree in mental health counseling from Nova Southeastern University. She lives in Raleigh, North Carolina, with her husband, Darrell, their two children, and a menagerie of animals. You can connect with Jen online at jenniferbleakley.com or on social media @jenbleakley.

Acknowledgments

WRITING BOOKS IS a big job that takes a lot of time and hard work, but it is also really, really fun! One of the most fun things about writing *Pawverbs for Kids* and *More Pawverbs for Kids* was thinking about you reading them! Every time I would sit down to write a story, I would imagine a kid—just like you—reading it, and that would make me smile. Then I would pet my dog, Gracie, and my cat, Foxy—who like to sit beside me while I type on my computer—and I would start to write a story, just for you.

So thank *you* for making this such a special book! I hope you like reading it as much as I liked writing it.

I also want to say a big thank you to some other special people who helped make this book:

Sarah Atkinson, thank you for coming to Raleigh all those years ago, for listening to me talk about the Pawverbs stories I had written for my kids, and suggesting I write them as a devotional series. These books would not exist if not for you!

Linda Howard, thank you for inviting me into the Tyndale Kids family! These books have been a dream come true for me—as is working with you!

Danika Kelly, it has been a joy to get to know and

work with you! Thank you for all of your work on these books. You are so talented, and these books are so much better because of you.

Ron Kaufmann, I can't imagine Pawverbs without you! Thank you so much for creating such gorgeous and special books. Pawverbs would not be the same without you.

A big thank you to Karen McGraw, Michelle Polsley, Natalie Wierenga, and Claire Lloyd. I am so honored to get to work with such an amazing (and downright PAWsome) team!

I also want to thank my friends Sarah and Carol for taking me to fun animal farms and for sending me funny texts and making me laugh while I worked on this book. And to my friends Aimee, Julie, Brooklyn, Tracy, Jodi G., Jodi S., Nicole, Barbara, and Sherri for giving me story ideas and always being there for me.

I want to say a big thank you to my mom and dad for loving me, praying for me, and helping me remember my own animal stories from when I was a kid. And to my Aunt Judy, for believing that I can do anything and for always being there for me.

Darrell, you are my safe place and my home. I couldn't do this without your support.

Andrew and Ella, never forget that Pawverbs started with you! Andrew, thank you for introducing the Paws family into our lives. It's so amazing to think how God was planting the seeds for these books all the way back then. Thank you both for letting me make up Pawverbs stories that summer when I forgot to pack your bedtime books. What I thought was a disaster, God used to make something really great. I started writing for you, and you will always be a part of everything I do.

And God, thank you for giving us such amazing animals that help us learn things about you. Thank you for letting me write these stories and thank you for loving me. Please let all my friends reading this book know that you love them and that you think they are really, really special.

Photography Credits

Unless otherwise noted, cover and interior photographs and illustrations are from Depositphotos and are the property of their respective copyright holders, and all rights are reserved. Listed by page number:

Front cover and spine . . . dog © Annette Shaff/Shutterstock

Front cover and spine . . . clouds © Janniwet Wangki

v. . . . . Ella and Andrew by Jennifer Bleakley, and used with permission

4 . . . . footprints background throughout © elisabetaaa

4 . . . . dog silhouette throughout © Anna Kaczor

5 . . . . birds throughout © Ekaterina Zirina

6, 8-9. . . . . . . girl with German shepherd © Andrii Sinenkyi

10 . . . . radiant cross throughout © Tyndale House Ministries

12 . . . . girl with puppy © Kosteniukova Natalii

13 . . . . squirrels throughout © MARIA Parafeynikova

16 . . . . horse head © RDNE Stock project/ Pexels

17, 95 . . . . . . horse silhouette © Aliaksandr Radzko

18 . . . . bee icons throughout © Antonina Yehanova

21 . . . . cat silhouette throughout © Jelena Amelconok

22 . . . . tortoises throughout © Anzhela Buch

22 . . . . sea turtles throughout © Svitlana Babych

23 . . . . cat bath © Nadezda Murmakova

27 . . . . boy with puppy © Mark Umbrella/Shutterstock

28-29. . . . . . . superhero and dog © Maxim Ibragimov/Shutterstock

30 . . . . salamander throughout © Polii/ Shutterstock

30 . . . . flat lizard throughout © alfadanz.stock.gmail.com

31 . . . . lizard throughout © Spreadthesign/Shutterstock

34 . . . . border collie in snow © by Tadeusz Lakota on Unsplash

38-39. . . . . . . boy and dog in snow © Cavan Images

40 . . . . sad golden retriever © Olga Prystai

44-45. . . . . . . Jack Russell under blanket © Javier Brosch/Shutterstock

50 . . . . kittens outside © by studioredcup on Freepik

53 . . . . girl with puppy in park © Dmytro Bandak

56 . . . . dog with red collar © by wirestock on Freepik

61 . . . . Asian girl kissing kitten © Ronnachai Palas/Shutterstock

64-65. . . . . . . girl playing with kittens © areetham/Shutterstock

67 . . . . buck silhouette © Elena Yotkova

68 . . . . reindeer in snow © SarahLou Photography/Shutterstock

72 . . . . girl in bed with cat © Iuliia Mashkov

76-77. . . . . . . girl with dog and cat © Iuliia Mashkov

79 . . . . bearded dragon silhouette © Sabina Rahimova

81 . . . . lizard on wood © by Ludwig Kwan on Pexels

84 . . . . African American girl with dog © Olga Yastremska

89 . . . . chicken silhouette © Khabib Alwi

90 . . . . smiling boy with chicken © Iuliia Gatcko/Shutterstock

94 . . . . girl with pony © Julza/Shutterstock

96-97 . . . . little girl and horse © Anya Melnikova/Shutterstock
103 . . . . girl in grass with puppy © Sawitree Pamee
106 . . . . dolphin and dog © Marie Blanton, and used with permission
110-111 . . . . . dog and dolphin © Nail Bikbaev/ Shutterstock
113 . . . . bird silhouette © Devon Carlson
114 . . . . bird by puddle © Muahmmad Nur Basri/Shutterstock
119 . . . . dog splashing in water © Rita_Kochmarjova/Shutterstock
122-123 . . . . . girl on beach with dog © NataSnow/Shutterstock
126 . . . . boy holding puppy © Anna Hoychuk/Shutterstock
130 . . . . girl petting dog © Shawn Hamilton/Shutterstock
134-135 . . . . . black girl hugging dog © Shawn Hamilton/Shutterstock
138 . . . . sleeping boy with dog © Irina Polonina/Shutterstock
142-143 . . . . . boy on bed hugs dog © Irina Polonina/Shutterstock
144 . . . . Portrait of a Boy with His Dog © Edgar Artiga/Masterfile
149 . . . . fish silhouette © Andrii Glushchenk
151 . . . . aquarium with Betta fish © Iryna Ennes
154-155 . . . . . girl with fishbowl © Deepak Sethi/iStockphoto
156 . . . . boy with black puppy © hartcreations/iStockphoto
162 . . . . Labrador holding toy © Alex Cooper Photography/Shutterstock
167 . . . . Asian girl with husky puppy © ANURAK PONGPATIMET/ Shutterstock
170-171 . . . . . girl and dog outside © S_Tanongsak/iStockphoto
175 . . . . Ella and a six-toed cat by Jennifer Bleakley, and used with permission
178 . . . . author with horse by Jennifer Bleakley, and used with permission

Back cover. . . African American girl with dog © fizkes/Shutterstock
Back cover. . . boy with chicken © Casey Jadew/ Shutterstock
Back cover. . . Portrait of a Boy with His Dog © Edgar Artiga/Masterfile
Back cover. . . girl playing with kittens © areetham/Shutterstock
Back cover. . . bee icons © Antonina Yehanova